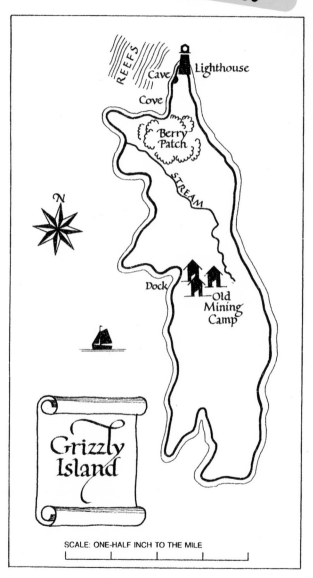

REEFS

Cave — Lighthouse

Cove

Berry Patch

STREAM

N

Dock

Old Mining Camp

Grizzly Island

SCALE: ONE-HALF INCH TO THE MILE

THE Carson KIDS and the Shipwreck on Grizzly Island

JAN PIERSON

AN AUTHORS GUILD BACKINPRINT.COM EDITION

AN AUTHORS GUILD BACKINPRINT.COM EDITION

Published by iUniverse.com, Inc.

For information address:
iUniverse.com, Inc.
620 North 48th Street, Suite 201
Lincoln, NE 68504-3467
www.iuniverse.com

Originally published by Tyndale House Publishers, Inc.

ISBN: 0-595-09072-9

Printed in the United States of America

To Julie with love

Contents

WARNING

RENEGADE GRIZZLY BEAR AT LARGE
ABSOLUTELY NO TRESPASSING
ON THIS ISLAND
BY ORDER OF THE
BRITISH COLUMBIA
DEPARTMENT OF WILDLIFE

One
Octopus Rocks

Blake and Jennifer Carson had been drifting for almost two days and nights in the unfamiliar waters when their battered skiff slammed into the rocks.

"Jump!" Blake yelled frantically, grabbing a jagged rock and trying to steady the floundering boat. "Hurry!" He felt the damaged craft splinter beneath his feet as he and his sister grabbed their rain-soaked gear and jumped to safety.

Breathless, Jennifer groped for solid footing on the slimy rocks. "This . . . this *is* an island, I hope!" she cried out in the darkness.

Blake shivered in the chill, hoping she was right, hoping they had found an island and not some reef stuck out in the middle of nowhere. The eerie warning of the whistle buoy had grown louder and louder, telling them they were nearing land. Or dangerous rocks. . . .

"Well?" Jennifer prodded, clinging to his jacket.

Blake didn't answer because he didn't know. His

thoughts were churning like the whirlpool that had just swallowed their boat. Bracing himself on the slippery rocks, he tried to get his bearings.

"If only there was a moon or a streetlight or *something!*" she rattled on, her brown hair flapping like wet seaweed in the wind.

Blake was fumbling for his flashlight, thankful that at least, they were still alive. They had been heading for Kwina Island when the storm barreled down from Canada without warning, hitting the San Juan Islands in unexpected fury. Submerged by sudden waves, their outboard motor went dead and they found themselves at the mercy of an angry sky and sea. His blue eyes flashed with fear as he flicked on his light, for he knew that even though the storm had passed, they were lost. They were stranded somewhere in a vast, unfamiliar archipelago of land and water.

"Hey, it *is* an island!" Her voice cut into his troubled thoughts. "Look!"

The chop and swell of the sea churned and sucked hungrily at his feet as he beamed his light toward the cliff rising like a fortress before them.

"Will you *please* say something?" she cried, moving carefully along the treacherous rock spit. "I'm getting sick and tired of doing all the talking!"

If the situation were not so critical right then, he might have laughed. But he didn't. He knew they had worse problems than her big mouth and one of them was a quickly rising tide that could swallow them up in minutes. They had to get to higher ground. And fast.

"We're not gonna be trapped, are we?" she

wailed, following him toward the forbidding wall of rock.

"That depends," he replied carefully.

"On what?"

"On which way the tide is moving," he went on, trying to hold his voice steady. He knew they had to find some protection for the night. A ledge. A cave. Anything. His trembling, frail beam of light searched the cliff, knowing that the threat of the creeping tide and exposure to cold were not the only dangers facing them. His breath came fast. *Octopuses lurked in rocks like these. . . .*

"Blake?" Jennifer's high-pitched voice cut into his grim thoughts.

"Yeah?"

"What's that?" She was pointing upward toward a yawning black crevice nearly hidden by a haze of salt spray from the churning surf.

Is it a cave? he wondered excitedly, trying to steady himself on the slimy rock path that was quickly being swallowed up by the sea. His body quivered with hope as he handed her his pack of camping gear and moved carefully toward the base of the cliff, then up the ragged wall of rock.

"Be careful!" she cried, watching him disappear into the black hole above her.

"We're in luck, Jen!" he called down, reaching for the gear, then her hand. "We're in luck. . . ."

Jennifer's teeth chattered with cold as she struggled up the cliff and over the slippery ledge where Blake now stood. "Wh . . . what is it?" she stammered, glancing furtively around.

"A cave."

"Oh, no!" she wailed. "No! I *hate* caves!"

Blake shook his head of wet blond hair in amazement. "I can't believe it, Jennifer."

"Can't believe what?"

"You!" He threw up his hands in disgust. "You mean to tell me you'd rather be down there on those rocks and freeze to death or get swallowed up by the tide or. . . ."

"Or . . . or what?" She gripped his wet jacket.

"Octopus," he said carefully.

"Octopus!" she burst out. "Blake, you've gotta be kidding!"

"No," he said grimly, kicking some broken glass and litter aside with his wet tennis shoe. "I'm not kidding."

Her chin dropped.

"If you want my opinion, we're darn lucky we found this place," he said as he collapsed on the uneven rock floor and began peeling off his jacket.

"*Who* found it?" She fell exhausted beside him and rolled her brown eyes heavenward.

"Yeah. OK, Jennifer. . . ."

"And it wasn't luck," she went on, struggling out of her soggy hooded sweatshirt.

Blake knew she was right. It *was* more than luck that had kept them afloat after the storm had hit the islands so unexpectedly. They had said good-bye to their folks on Gooseberry Island and were on their way to Kwina Island for a week of camping and picking apples on the Gribble's farm when it happened. But where had the wind and the tide and the waves carried them? And who would know they were missing?

"Don't you think Mom and Dad will check to make sure we got to the Gribbles?" Jennifer asked finally. "Maybe they got worried when the storm hit."

He gave her a sour look. "I've already told you. How can they do that if there aren't any phones on Kwina Island?"

She sighed. "Yeah, I know, but maybe Mom and Dad will take the boat over just to check and make sure we made it."

"What boat?" he snorted, wondering how she could forget that the only boat the Carson family owned was now sitting in a saltwater grave somewhere off this reef. "And if you'll remember," he went on, "the Gribbles didn't know we were coming for sure. Their letter just invited us to come over and camp and pick apples sometime before school started."

"So maybe nobody knows we're missing?" she asked gravely.

He didn't answer because he feared she might be right.

"But sooner or later, *somebody's* gotta find out, don't they, Blake?"

"Sure," he said thickly, holding back the creeping fear that by that time it might be too late.

"Like that time we got stranded over on Five Finger Island, remember?" Her words were coming too fast. "They found us then. . . ."

Blake reached for his waterproof pack that had kept out most of the rain and pulled out his sleeping bag. "Let's get some sleep," he said, changing the subject. "I'm bushed."

"Sleep?" She grabbed the flashlight and shined it around on the glazed rock walls encircling them.

15

"Who's gonna sleep in a creepy place like this?"

"Me," he replied, laying his sleeping bag carefully on the uneven floor. He was exhausted. They had scarcely slept since this crazy adventure started two days before.

"Well I won't sleep a wink," she muttered, spreading out her sleeping bag beside him and flicking out the light. She peeled out of her damp outer clothing and crawled into her uncomfortable bed. "Not a wink."

Blake just grunted. He was thankful to be alive.

"I wonder where we are?" she asked, blinking wide-eyed in the darkness.

"In a cave, dummy."

"That's not what I mean. . . ."

Blake sighed. "Who knows? Since yesterday, I haven't recognized any of these islands."

"You don't think maybe we've drifted out into the Pacific Ocean or something horrible like that, do you?" she went on in a worried tone.

"No, but I think we might have been carried north into Canadian waters."

"You mean the Gulf Islands?"

"Maybe."

"But, there are hundreds of those islands, Blake! And if we are off the northern coast of British Columbia, who'll ever find us? I mean, we might as well be lost in the Yukon!"

Blake felt a chill, knowing she was probably right. Anyway, he didn't want to think about it right then. He was so tired. So very tired. . . .

"And along with everything else, this has got to be the most uncomfortable bed I have ever slept on," she muttered. "I feel like I'm sleeping on nails."

He pulled his sleeping bag over his head.

"And I'm also hungry and wet and cold to the bone," she went on grimly, "and who knows what might be crawling around in here! Blake? Blake, did you hear me?"

Her brother didn't reply. He was praying that his sister would be quiet so he could get some sleep. And thankfully, his prayers were answered because the next thing he knew, it was morning.

"Wake up!" Jennifer was tugging on his arm. "The tide's out and I think there's a little cove just around the headland. Hurry!"

Blake blinked in the pall of fog that had filtered into the cave, listening to a foghorn buoy drone monotonously somewhere in the waters beyond.

"Come on!" she said, hurrying back over to the mouth of the cave and straining through the gray haze. "Hurry up before the tide changes and we get trapped in this dumb cave again."

He was up and ready to go almost before she had reached the base of the cliff directly below the cave. "Here, catch!" he called down, tossing her the gear.

Arms loaded, Jennifer waited as he climbed down the sharp stepway onto the barnacled rock that was now exposed by the low tide.

Blake whistled softly, staring at the jagged reef stretching out like sharks' teeth into the foggy haze. "No wonder we crash landed," he said to her. "I'll bet this place has been a graveyard for more than just our boat!"

She handed him his pack, then started along the base of the cliff toward the cove. "Yeah, I'll bet that's why we heard that awful wailing whistle buoy last night."

"Yeah, except with reefs like this, there should be more than just warning buoys and foghorns," he said, stepping carefully over starfish and tide pools and bright-colored anemones. "There should be a lighthouse."

Jennifer reached the cove first. "Well, I'll be darned!" she called to him. "There is!"

"Huh?" He leaped off the rocky headland and landed on the small pebbled beach.

"There *is* a lighthouse!" She was pointing excitedly. "Look!"

Blake shook his head in amazement, staring through the haze of fog at the old wooden structure standing alone on the spit of land jutting into the sea. "What do you know?" he laughed. "Our cave must have been almost directly below it!"

Gulls, feeding on the beach, scattered and flew into the fog as Jennifer hurried across the cove and climbed the low bank.

"Maybe we can send a signal from the tower." His voice brimmed with hope as he followed her.

But his sister wasn't listening. She had stopped on the ridge above him, as though frozen to the rock.

"What's wrong?" He scrambled up behind her, wondering why she had turned as pale as the white gulls that had flown into the mist.

And then he knew. Blake's heart nearly stopped

as he stared at the freshly stenciled sign that had been rammed into the hard earth:

WARNING
RENEGADE GRIZZLY BEAR AT LARGE
ABSOLUTELY NO TRESPASSING ON THIS ISLAND
BY ORDER OF THE
BRITISH COLUMBIA DEPARTMENT OF WILDLIFE

Two
The Lonely Lighthouse

A long-necked cormorant launched itself like a black phantom from the tower as Blake and Jennifer raced like sandpipers toward the old wooden lighthouse. Except for a few run-down outbuildings and wind-battered trees, the spit was barren. Desolate.

They were nearly out of breath when they reached the apparently deserted structure. Blake hesitated. The ancient, cone-shaped building looked to him as though it might collapse in the next big wind.

Jennifer was the first inside. Breathless, she struggled like a wild thing, trying to bolt the wobbly door behind them.

"Hey, take it easy!" He grabbed her trembling arm.

"But . . . a *grizzly!*" Jennifer paled, shaking like a juniper in the wind. "On this island! Oh, Blake . . ."

"We'll be safe in here," he told her, but as he

glanced around, he wondered. The place looked about ready to fall apart. The once whitewashed walls and floors were peeling and rotted and the panes of glass in the small windows were shattered. A faint, eerie wind whistled down from the light gallery above. Blake gripped the railing at the foot of the balustrade, knowing they wouldn't be sending any signal from this old tower. Or what was left of it. It looked to him as if this old place had been defying the threats of the wind and sea for years—and now the battle was almost over.

"Will you *please* help me board up these windows?" Jennifer cut into his thoughts with her high-pitched voice. She was scurrying around like a frantic squirrel, picking up planks and boards. "And the door, Blake! It's ready to fall off its hinges. We've gotta brace it somehow. Bolt it!"

"Just cool it, Jennifer. OK?"

She stopped in her tracks, then nodded. "Yeah, I guess you're right."

"There's no grizzly in this lighthouse, and if we use our heads, there isn't going to be, either." She nodded again, then let out a yell.

"What's wrong?" Blake reeled around to face his terror-stricken sister.

"Yuck!" She drew back. "Mice! Horrible dead little mice all over this place! Look!" She was standing beneath the old staircase, pointing clumsily with a plank.

"Good grief, Jennifer." Blake walked over and kicked aside a tiny carcass in disgust.

"Well, I'm not sleeping in this place, I can tell you that," she huffed. "Not with these creepy little things running around. No way!"

22

"You prefer grizzlies then?" he snorted.

"It's not funny."

"I know," he said grimly, taking the plank from her hand and pulling out a square pegged nail.

"What're you doing?" She made a face.

Blake was examining the rusty spike. "This thing is old. . . ."

"I know," she said nervously. "Just like everything else around here. This place is falling in."

"Not quite," he replied, "but it'll do until we figure out what to do next."

Jennifer shot a wary glance up the old staircase toward the gallery, where a lighted lantern once flashed its warnings. "I s'pose it won't work, huh." she said flatly, pointing to the old lens and reflector overhead. "I mean, we can't signal for help with that beat-up old thing, can we?"

"Not unless you can round up some lard oil," Blake replied, stepping past her and moving carefully up the winding balustrade, testing each step before he put his weight on it.

"Lard oil? You mean this lighthouse is that old?"

"Well, maybe kerosene," he called down to her. "But this place *is* old. I'll bet it was built way before the turn of the century. You don't see very many like this. These wooden jobs never held up, so they finally started making them out of stone and brick and stuff." He turned and circled on up toward the tower.

"Be careful," she said, glancing back at the door she had braced shut with a plank. "I'd hate to lose you now."

When Blake reached the top, he gripped the railing and stepped carefully onto the uneven floor of the gallery. Most of the glass encircling the old tower had been shattered by the constant winds and storms, and the lantern was rusted and crumbling with age. Even though the fog was beginning to lift and a few shafts of late summer sun filtered through the remaining panes of glass, he felt a chill. *Not even lard oil is going to help this old thing.* Discouraged, he turned and started back down the staircase, knowing they would have to find some other way to signal for help.

They spent the rest of the morning boarding up the windows and securing the old place as best they could. Their damp packs and some outer clothing were hanging in the breezy gallery to dry.

"I'm hungry, Blake," she said finally, wiping her dusty face with the sleeve of her sweatshirt. "I can't believe we ate all three batches of those cookies Mom packed for us to take to the Gribbles. But they're gone. One hundred and eighty chocolate chip cookies, four sandwiches and the bananas have all been wiped out."

"Yeah," he said blankly. His growling stomach had already been reminding him that there was nothing left but a trickle of water in his canteen.

"Well? What're we going to do?"

"We won't starve, if that's what you mean," he said, sitting down on the uneven floor. "There are plenty of fish and clams out there, and I'll bet this island is covered with berries."

Her eyes widened. "Are you going out there and get 'em?"

"We'll just have to be careful, that's all."

She collapsed on the floor beside him. *"We?"*

"Yeah, Jennifer," he said with a sigh.

"Well, *I'm* not going berry-picking or clam-digging with a grizzly bear running around, I can tell you that. I'll eat boards first!"

"Don't be stupid. We don't even know where that bear is. Maybe this island is fifty miles long, and maybe he's at the other end."

"And maybe he isn't."

"We have to eat," Blake reminded her.

"And so does he," she said grimly.

Unfortunately he knew his sister was probably right for a change, but they had to eat, didn't they? If they didn't do something, they'd shrivel up and die like those little mice under the staircase. He felt a chill.

"What're we gonna do?" She cut into his gruesome thoughts. "We just have to get out of here, Blake. We have to get off this island!"

"And how do you suggest we do that?" he asked dryly.

"Will you please quit changing the subject!"

"Huh?"

"I told you I was hungry."

Blake shook his head. She was hopeless, wasn't she? Completely hopeless.

"Well?" she prodded.

"It's up to you, Jennifer."

"Me? What're you talking about?"

"What'll it be? Boards or berries?"

She stood up slowly, smoothing the creases in her faded jeans. "Yeah, well, OK. . . ."

25

Blake found an old coffee can for the berries, then picked up his canteen. "I hope we can find some water," he said.

Jennifer was already peering out a knothole.

"Well?" He moved the plank securing the old door.

"Well, what?" she faltered.

"All clear?"

"How . . . how do I know?" Her voice was quavering.

Blake rolled his eyes, then carefully opened the door. "It's bare," he said, gazing around.

"It's a *what?*" she cried out, slamming the door shut in his face.

"I said it's bare," he snorted. "Nothing's out there."

Jennifer's eyes were as round as the knothole. "I . . . I thought you said. . . ."

Blake started laughing.

"It's not funny," she said hotly.

Blake bit his lip, figuring it wasn't the time to get into another stupid argument. Regaining control, he opened the door once more, then motioned for her to follow.

"Be sure to tell me if you see or hear anything," she rattled, staying close to his heels. "*Anything.* And remember. . . ."

"Jennifer." He held down his voice. "How can I hear if you keep babbling? Just keep your eyes and ears open and your mouth shut. OK?"

She muttered something under her breath as she followed him across the spit and into the trees beyond. Fir and pine and hemlock encircled them suddenly.

26

Finally they reached a clearing where a fence of low-growing bushes surrounded a little meadow. Sparrows and towhees and juncos chattered noisily in the branches overhead as they crept toward the bushes laden with bright red salmonberries. In minutes, they were both eating hungrily and filling the can with the fruit.

Suddenly their feast was cut short by a sharp sound in the thicket beyond. It seemed as though even the birds froze in the branches above.

"What's that?" Jennifer whirled around.

"I . . . I don't know," Blake choked, grabbing the can of berries and taking off for the lighthouse. "Just run, Jennifer! Run as fast as you can!"

Three
A Cat Stalks

The sagging door of the lighthouse almost fell off
its hinges when they slammed it shut behind them
and shoved the plank into place. Blake's heart was
thudding like a hammer as he peered out the
knothole to see if they were being pursued.

"Is . . . is . . . ?" Jennifer was breathless.
Petrified.

"No," he replied thankfully. "He . . . it . . .
there's nothing out there. Nothing."

Jennifer took the can of berries from his
trembling hands and sighed in relief.

"Probably just a deer or coon," he said carefully,
knowing she'd be scared half out of her wits if she
could read his grim thoughts right then.

"*Or* a grizzly." She held his wide gaze.

"I didn't say that."

"But that's what you're thinking, isn't it?"

"It could be anything, Jennifer," he said thickly.
"A brown bear, a cat—anything."

"*Cat!*" she gasped.

"Sure," he shrugged. "Animals swim back and forth between islands all the time."

Jennifer threw her berry-stained hand against her head and moaned. "First a grizzly and now maybe bobcats or cougars or—"

"It was probably just a coon," he interrupted. But he knew by the look on her face that she wasn't convinced.

And neither was he. The threat of the powerful grizzly hung like a storm cloud as they both hustled around, trying to secure the old building for the night coming all too soon. Blake hoped his sister was unaware that the only natural enemy of the grizzly was man and that it would attack almost anything when hungry or startled. But he also knew grizzlies had poor eyesight and depended mostly on their sense of smell. So if this one had not caught their scent—or if it was actually some smaller animal—they were probably safe. But if it *was* a grizzly they had heard, he doubted that even a run-down old lighthouse could keep it out.

He wished that one of the smaller outbuildings had still been intact—the lightkeeper's house, the foghorn house, anything but this drafty old place that threatened to blow down in the next big wind.

Blake's uneasiness grew as darkness covered the island and they bedded down for the night. He knew that his own five-foot-nine frame was scarcely a match for a creature that sometimes grew as tall as eight feet and weighed as much as nine hundred pounds. Besides that, the eerie wailing of the wind in the tower and the branches scraping the wall outside weren't helping his state of mind. And then it hit him. *Branches scraping the wall? There weren't any branches outside. . . .*

"What's that weird noise?" Jennifer's razor-edged voice cut into his uneasy thoughts.

"Just . . . the wind," he said carefully, groping for his flashlight and the plank.

"No. . . ." She grabbed his arm in the shroud of darkness. "It's something else. Scraping. Clawing. . . ." Her voice faltered.

She was right, he knew. There was something outside. Something crawling up the back side of the lighthouse.

"We didn't even think of boarding up the windows in the tower," she whispered thickly. "Oh, Blake. . . ."

His knuckles whitened as he held the flashlight in one hand—the plank in the other.

"Blake!" she wailed.

"Shhh!" he ordered, creeping across his sleeping bag toward the eerie sound merging with the wailing wind.

"No!" She grabbed the hem of his jeans. "Don't, Blake! Don't go up there!"

Unheeding, he crawled like a weasel past her, listening to the eerie sound grow louder and louder. A cold sweat crept down his spine as he slowly, carefully moved up the old staircase. Suddenly, except for the wailing of the wind, it was quiet.

"Blake, no!" Jennifer's raw whisper broke into his frenzied thoughts. "It's there now, isn't it? She was running toward the foot of the balustrade, gesturing wildly at her brother on the shadowy staircase above her. "Be careful!"

Dizzy with fear, he braced himself at the top of the landing, then flicked on his flashlight. The trembling light in his hand moved slowly upward, then stopped as it caught the iridescent glow of two eyes.

The glaring yellow eyes of a cat.

Four
Miss Pearl Gray

The creature leaped from a broken window frame onto the gallery floor.

"What?" Jennifer cried, unbelieving. "It's only a cat, Blake! A little gray kitty cat!"

Her brother was so overcome with relief that all he could do was laugh. He couldn't stop.

"Here, kitty, kitty, kitty." Jennifer called softly as she moved slowly up the balustrade. "Don't be afraid. We won't hurt you."

The gray ball of fluff sauntered like royalty down the rickety stairs toward her, as though it were descending a polished mahogany staircase in the royal palace. A silver tag was attached to its tiny collar and flashed in the pale light.

"You poor, scared little thing," Jennifer murmured, scooping up the cat. "We boarded up your house so you couldn't get in, could you?" she said gently, stroking the soft gray fur. "Well, it's all right now. You don't need to be afraid anymore."

Afraid? Blake held back his grin as he came

down the steps. He knew who really had been afraid.

"Poor little thing is probably starving, too," Jennifer went on.

"Starving? Are you kidding?" He walked up and stroked the opalescent fur. "He or she or whatever it is looks as fat as a seal!"

"Yeah, I guess you're right," his sister muttered, trying to read the tag jangling from the collar. "Maybe just abandoned, huh?"

He shrugged.

Jennifer took the flashlight from his hand and directed its beam at the silver tag. "Pearl Gray," she repeated slowly, then looked up. "And then there's this number right below her name."

"Well, Miss Pearl Gray," Blake smiled, returning to his bed, "we know your name and your license number but we don't know where you came from, do we?"

The cat responded with a rickety sort of meow and followed them to their sleeping bags. She was purring like a well-tuned outboard motor.

"You don't suppose she lives on this island, do you?" Jennifer asked, lying back in the shadows once again. "Maybe there's a house or cabin nearby."

"I doubt it," he replied. "Not with a ritzy collar and name like that. No, I'd say she probably came off somebody's fancy cruiser while they were picnicking in a cove or something like that. And you can see she's not starving, so it's likely it wasn't very long ago, either."

"Maybe you're right," Jennifer answered. "Unless she got left at somebody's summer cabin by mistake. Maybe the owners couldn't find her when it was time to leave."

"Could be," Blake replied, gritting his teeth while the cat's claws busily massaged his thighs. "We haven't really explored the island yet. Maybe there *is* a cabin somewhere—maybe even a boat moored in somebody's cove."

"Explored?" she said weakly. "What do you mean, we haven't explored this island yet? Who's going exploring with a grizzly running around?"

"We have to do something, Jennifer," he said, knowing they couldn't live on berries for long. Besides that, his nervous system would not stand too many more nights like these last two. He placed the vibrating Miss Gray at the foot of Jennifer's sleeping bag and scrunched back down in his bed. "Let's talk about it in the morning. We've gotta get some sleep."

For a change his sister was quiet, and even though the wind was still whistling in the tower, somehow everything seemed a little bit better. Miss Gray was totally at ease with the whole situation, so why shouldn't they be, too? Blake closed his heavy lids and was soon fast asleep.

Bright and early the next morning, he was awakened by Jennifer's ear-splitting shrieks.

"What now?" he groaned.

And then he understood. Miss Gray was dragging a very dead rat across Jennifer's sleeping bag.

"Get it *out!*" Her muffled shrieks were still audible, even from inside her sleeping bag. "OUT!"

"Sorry, Miss Gray," Blake snickered, opening the

door a crack and ushering the cat and her prize outside, "but you'd better keep your toys out of here from now on."

"Is it gone?" Jennifer asked grimly, poking her nose out of her bed.

"Yup," he said, slipping on his shirt. "We'll survive."

Disheveled, Jennifer crawled out of her sleeping bag and moaned. "We've gotta find a way off this island soon, Blake. I can't stand this much longer. Dead rats and caves and this dumb lighthouse that sounds like it's got ghosts in the tower! And a grizzly besides. . . ."

"We'll find a way," he assured her. "Somehow."

"But how?"

"First by finding out whether there is a boat or cabin somewhere on this island," he told her.

"But the *grizzly!*"

"Maybe there isn't a grizzly, Jennifer," he said, hoping to get her mind off the bear.

"Huh?"

He cleared his throat. "Uh, animals swim from island to island all the time. Maybe he swam to the next island."

"What island?" She gave him a sour look. "I haven't seen any islands around here, have you?"

She was right. It was a weak argument, he knew. "Well, it doesn't matter anyway," he said, picking up his canteen and the coffee can they had emptied for dinner the night before. "I think grizzlies are poor swimmers."

"Then how did it get here in the first place?" she persisted.

Blake gave her a blank look. He hadn't even thought about that. "Jennifer—"

"All right, if we *have* to explore this dumb island, let's get it over with," she interrupted. "But let's hike along the shoreline—stay on the beaches as much as we can."

"Huh?"

"If grizzlies are poor swimmers, then that probably means they don't like water, right?"

"Yeah, well maybe," he replied, tying his tennis shoes.

"So we stay out of meadows and berry patches and. . . ."

"Jennifer," he said, walking over to the door and motioning her out, "we have to get water and more of those berries just in case we get stuck on this island longer than we expect. There's gotta be a creek or a stream somewhere."

"No way!" She shook her tousled head firmly. "I'm *not* going back to that berry patch with—"

"With a kitty cat lurking in the bushes?" he said dryly. "Now, grab your canteen and let's go."

"It still *could* have been that bear," she grumbled, following him across the barren spit and into the trees.

"But I don't think it was."

"Are you sure?" She glanced around nervously, unconvinced.

"Almost," he replied, plodding through the thick ground cover of fern and salal and wild vine. "Last night after I got my head on straight, I realized we hadn't seen any bear signs around here. No slashes on the tree bark, no droppings, nothing. If it wasn't the cat we heard in the meadow, then it was probably just a coon or deer."

"I hope you're right." She gulped.

Blake hoped so, too.

At last they reached the clearing where they had found the berries the day before. Blake's eyes darted around like a hawk's. Except for a warm morning sun filtering through the trees, the meadow was empty. He breathed a deep sigh of relief.

The fresh blend of sea and shore filled the air as they began to fill the can and their mouths with berries. "I've been thinking," he said to his sister finally. "In case this little vacation drags on longer than we'd like, we're going to need more than just berries to keep us going."

Jennifer turned to him, her cheeks stuffed like a chipmunk's pouch with the sweet fruit. "No!" she almost choked. "It can't!"

"But just in case it does, I think I can get some rockfish near that kelp bed offshore."

"We'll find something," she put in quickly, wiping some red juice off her quivering chin. "A cabin, a boat, something!"

Blake hoped she was right, but he had a strong feeling this island was deserted. He remembered the government warning sign and knew that nobody with any brains would be hanging around with a grizzly running loose. But just in case there did happen to be an empty cabin somewhere, he knew they would be a lot safer there than in the lighthouse. And if they did find a cabin, then maybe there would be a boathouse, too. And a boat. A faint hope rose within him as he helped

Jennifer finish filling the can with berries.

They left the can at the edge of the clearing, intending to pick it up on the way back to the lighthouse. He knew the next thing they must do was find water.

Ragged nettles stung their arms and ankles as they moved carefully through the underbrush. Watching. Listening.

"What about a signal fire after dark?" Jennifer asked finally, pausing to rest against a huge Douglas fir.

"Signal who?"

"Gee, Blake—sooner or later there has to be a boat coming near the island, doesn't there? At least we could be ready." She brushed a straggle of chestnut brown hair from her worried brow.

"Maybe," he agreed, starting out through the heavy undergrowth once more. "But if we don't find some water before long, it won't matter."

Jennifer drew a sudden breath, then followed him through the thick tangle of late-summer greens and golds. Time dragged like a sluggish tide but at last they found a creek. Overjoyed, Blake and Jennifer sloshed and rollicked around like a couple of carefree ducks in the cool, refreshing stream of water. It felt wonderful on their hot, salt-crusted skin and quenched their nagging thirst.

After they had filled their canteens, they moved back toward the sound of the sea, hoping to find a cabin or boat along the shoreline. Jennifer's heart nearly stopped every time she heard an unfamiliar sound or snap of a twig and when they reached the edge of the island, her hopes of trekking the rest of the way along the beach were dashed. The high ridge dropped a hundred feet to the sharp rocks below.

She sighed and followed her brother through the ragged juniper and pungent Scotch broom edging the cliff, zigzagging like crazy loons over the rough terrain. The sun felt good against the cool salt wind coming off the water as they hiked southward down a gradual incline.

Jennifer had moved ahead and was standing on an arm of land when she saw the cove and old dock. "Hey!" she yelled excitedly. "Look at that!"

"Well, I'll be!" he cried, when he saw the natural harbor almost hidden in the arc of rock and earth. But when they reached the cove, he saw that, except for the run-down dock, there were no other buildings in sight. Not a house or a cabin anywhere. Nothing except another one of those signs, warning people to keep off the island.

"Phooey!" he snorted, kicking a can in his path.

Jennifer walked over and picked up the can, then gave him a curious look.

"What's the matter?" he asked flatly.

"It's not rusty and old like everything else on this island."

"So?"

"So maybe that's because somebody has been here. Recently," she said carefully. "And look over there," she went on, pointing to a slightly trampled path that led into the trees. "Squirrels don't trample down the underbrush like that, do they Blake?"

No, he thought grimly, his wide blue eyes searching the trees for slash marks on the bark, *but grizzlies do.*

"Come on!" she called, beckoning with the shiny can. "This might lead us to a house or a cabin!"

Blake hoped she was right.

Five
Pot of Gold?

Blake saw the shack first. It was nearly hidden by the wild, rambling blackberry vines and when he got closer, he saw that there were more old buildings just like it scattered around.

"A mining camp, maybe?" Jennifer whispered, staring at the ramshackle remains of the cabins and mineshafts. She moved ahead on the trail, brushing some litter and branches aside with a large stick she had picked up along the way.

He nodded, explaining what Salty Bob had told him about the men who had tried to mine for gold and silver and copper in these islands a long time ago. "But I guess the ore was low grade and too hard to transport so they gave up and went after timber instead," he said to her. *"Green gold is all these islands will ever yield,"* the old fisherman friend had told him. *"The rich green gold of timber."*

Jennifer moved toward the shack, brushing aside some more litter with her stick. "With all this garbage, there's gotta be somebody—"

Before she could finish, the trail in front of her exploded in a thundering clash of steel. Jennifer was thrown backward, her stick ripped from her hand and snapped in two by powerful jaws of steel.

"Wh . . . what?" she sputtered, brushing the leaves and branches from her trembling frame. "What happened?"

"A trap," Blake said soberly, staring at the huge metal clamps that had almost caught his sister in a death grip.

"T . . . trap?"

"Yeah, a bear trap."

"You mean for the grizzly?" Her eyes were as round as the sun that was now beginning to drop in the sky.

He nodded nervously, peering around the deserted camp, then crouching down and examining the deadly steel teeth more closely. *We were warned by those signs, weren't we?*

"Good thing I had my stick, huh?" Her words cut into his uneasy thoughts.

He nodded vaguely, wiping the sudden rush of sweat from his brow. It was a close call, he knew. Too close. And yet, they were OK, weren't they? Nobody was hurt. A sudden, unexpected thanks to God welled up inside of him as he got up and turned his gaze into the late afternoon sky. *"Thanks,"* he said quietly. *"Thanks a lot."*

"You're welcome," his sister replied, picking up another stick and handing it to him.

"Jennifer. . . ."

"Mmmmm?" She walked off, pounding the trail with another stick.

Blake shrugged hopelessly, then followed her around the trap and into the vine-encroached clearing. He felt like a blind man with a cane as he moved slowly with his prodding, poking stick. Gunnysacks and jugs and shovels were littered around or propped against the old buildings and sheds ravaged by time. Then Blake noticed one building that looked different, sturdier than the rest. Skirting a wheelbarrow, he motioned for Jennifer to follow him.

She stayed close to her brother's heels as they moved along the half-trampled path to a slatted wooden door hanging ajar. A huge machete was propped against the wall. "Ugh!" she gasped, staring at the gigantic blade glistening in the sun. "Let's get out of this creepy place!"

But Blake was already peering curiously inside.

"Anybody home?" Jennifer whispered, glancing over his shoulder.

"Not right now," he replied carefully. But he knew someone had been there and it was not very long ago, either. The momentarily unoccupied living quarters were a mess. Beer cans and cigarette butts lay like dead flies on the rotting wood floor, and the stench of garbage was nauseating.

"Yuck, it stinks!" Jennifer drew back with a grimace.

"You're telling me," he said, backing away slowly.

"I mean it *really* stinks in there, Blake. It's weird. Different from anything I've ever smelled before."

"Well, something around here sure is weird," he

agreed, making quick tracks away from the vile place. And he had no intention of finding out what it was, either.

"Blake?" Jennifer called out. "What's this?"

He turned and saw her peering into a tunnel of briar.

"Come on," she motioned, crouching down and disappearing into the hand-hewn passage of blackberry vines.

"What next?" he muttered, following her.

And when they reached the end of the tunnel, his question was answered. Jennifer was standing at the edge of a huge field of green stalks that waved gently in the late afternoon breeze.

"Well, I'll be darned," she sighed. "A big garden."

"Jen . . . Jennifer. . . ." He struggled to speak. "Don't you know what that is?"

"Smells like tea or spices or something," she went on, unfastening the canteen from her belt and taking a long, refreshing drink. Setting her canteen on the ground, she reached toward a budding stalk that was taller than she was. "I wonder. . . ."

Blake drew back, knowing exactly what the plant was. *Exactly!* But before he could tell her, he heard a sound in the distance. Branches breaking on the trail. Voices. Someone was coming!

"What's wrong?" Jennifer whirled around.

"We've gotta get outta here!" he choked, his eyes darting quickly around the fence of vines encircling them.

"Why?"

"Don't argue, just follow me and keep quiet!"

he ordered, frantically searching for some way out.

At last he found a space large enough for them to crawl through. "Hurry!" he motioned impatiently, diving into the break in the wall of thorns.

"But, I don't understand," she muttered, vines and briars tearing at her face and clothing. "This is dumb!"

"It's worse than that," he whispered hoarsely, breaking out into the open and leaping across logs and stumps until they had reached the protection of the trees.

"Now," she said with breathless impatience, "will you please tell me what's going on?" Her clothes were filthy and torn, her skin scratched and bleeding. "And you'd better come up with something good, too!"

"Yeah," he said, grabbing a large stick and beating a trail once more. "I'll tell you as soon as we put some distance between us and that little farm back there."

Still complaining, she stumbled behind him, struggling against the heavy undergrowth. At last they reached the other shore, where great rock cliffs hung like shrouds against the formless sea beyond. Blake collapsed against a tree, breathless but thankful they hadn't run into any more traps. And he was almost sure no one had followed them.

"Well?" Jennifer asked.

"Well, what?" he said absently, wiping the salty sweat off his scratched, stinging arms.

"How come we've been running like a couple of crazy loons?"

"Didn't you hear them?" he asked. "The voices?"

The color drained from her face. "You mean back at that garden?"

He nodded stiffly.

"Maybe it's just the guys who live there." She smiled tightly. "Maybe they're just a couple of nice old farmers—"

"Jennifer," he said, realizing she still failed to recognize what they had just discovered. "Don't you—"

"And just because they're lousy housekeepers doesn't mean—"

"Jennifer," he said again, shaking his head in disbelief, "maybe you're right about their being farmers, but they may not be old and they probably aren't nice."

"Huh?" She wrinkled her upturned nose.

"Didn't you notice something odd about that crop those guys were cultivating?"

She shook her head, perplexed. "You mean those funny little maplely trees?"

"Jennifer, how can you be so *dumb?*"

She made a face. "What're you talking about?"

"I'm talking about what we just stumbled on."

She cocked her head curiously. "Yeah?"

"A pot farm, Jennifer."

"A what?"

He drew a tolerant sigh, then spoke again. "Those funny little maple trees just happen to be a very large crop of marijuana!"

"Marijuana?" She almost fell over backward. "You're kidding!"

"No, I'm not kidding. When I first saw those

48

plastic jugs and buckets and stuff lying around, I began to wonder," he explained.

"Jugs?"

"Yeah," he replied. "For fertilizer. And the buckets must have been for water. Irrigating. The creek was somewhere nearby. I heard it."

"And that horrible knife?" She was wide-eyed now.

"A machete," he said, glancing furtively around. "Probably for cutting down the stalks when it's time for the harvest. And I'll bet they use some of those sheds for drying the stuff, too," he went on.

"How come you know so much?"

"I was going to ask you the same thing, only in reverse. I mean, Jennifer, we may live on an island but not everybody's got their head stuck in the sand! Don't you ever read the newspapers? Hasn't the sheriff ever come and talked to your class?"

"I'm sorry I asked," she sighed, rolling her eyes heavenward. "So what now?"

"Now we make tracks back to the lighthouse," he replied, unfastening his canteen from his belt and taking a drink.

"But are you sure they weren't following us?" She glanced into the trees.

"Almost positive. For all they know, the only threat on this island is that grizzly. Now grab your canteen and let's go."

Jennifer gasped.

"What's the matter?" His voice was edged with impatience as he hooked his canteen back onto his belt loop.

"Well, uh—see, I think maybe—we've got a problem."

"Problem?" He turned to his sister who had turned as white as the foam lining the beach below.

She nodded dumbly.

"Well?" he prodded impatiently. "What is it, Jennifer?"

"My canteen."

"What about your canteen?"

"Uh. . . ." She licked her dry lips and spoke carefully. "I left it back there."

"Back *where?*" His throat felt suddenly dry.

"Back by those weird little maple trees," she said weakly. "Gee, Blake, I just set it down after I had a drink. . . ."

His heart fell like a rock. "No, Jennifer. No. . . ."

Six
Secret Passage

"Well, I didn't do it on *purpose!*" she said hotly.

"Jennifer, you never do things on purpose," he shot back, his sweaty hand gripping his stick so tightly his knuckles were white. "They just happen, don't they? Crazy things like this *always* happen whenever you're around!"

She charged past him with her stick, beating a trail with sudden vengeance. "You'll be glad I came," she snorted. "You'll be thanking me. You just wait!"

"Sure, Jennifer," he muttered, moving past her on the overgrown path. It was hopeless trying to argue with her, anyway. Totally hopeless. And now, thanks to her, they were really in a fix. It was just a matter of time before the men would discover the canteen and be hot on their trail. And, he thought grimly, the lighthouse was bound to be one of the first places they would probably look. Blake knew he and his sister were going to have to find another place to hide.

Blake stepped up his pace, wondering how long it would take them to reach the lighthouse from this side of the island. The sun was dropping quickly behind the trees on the western horizon and without jackets, they were both beginning to feel the chill. But he knew that if they moved steadily north, they would reach it eventually and his growling stomach was reminding him not to forget the can of berries they had left in the meadow.

When they saw the lighthouse in the far distance at last, they both felt a huge load had been lifted from their shoulders, for darkness was now almost upon them. At least there had been no more traps and with the darkness came the hope that they were probably safe for the night at least. *But after that—for how long?* Blake wondered uneasily, cutting inland toward the meadow where their meager fare of berries for dinner was waiting.

"Where is she?" Jennifer said the moment they had bolted the old door of the lighthouse behind them.

"She?" Blake was already stuffing his mouth hungrily with the berries.

"Miss Gray. She's not here," she said, reaching for the can. "Here, kitty, kitty, kitty. . . ."

"Miss Gray?" Blake shook his head in disbelief. "Jennifer. . . ."

"Maybe she got upset when you sent her out this morning," she went on worriedly.

Her brother was still shaking his head in amazement. "I can't believe it, Jennifer," he said, reaching for more berries. "Here we are, stranded, our lives may be in danger—and you're worried about that cat!"

"Maybe she won't come back," she said, handing him the can and walking over to search beneath the balustrade. "She could be lost. Here, kitty, kitty. . . ."

"Jennifer," he said sharply, "Miss Gray is going to be fine. It's *us* I'm worried about!"

But she was not impressed, and her concern grew as they prepared to settle down for the night.

His sister was really beginning to get on his nerves, and if it hadn't been that she'd accidently found a stash of candy bars in her pack, he might have been tempted to stuff her down a large knothole. But now they both knew she held a certain power over him.

"You don't think the grizzly got Miss Gray, do you?" Jennifer asked dismally, crawling into her sleeping bag. "Or maybe she got trapped in a crevice?"

He wiped some chocolate from his mouth and tried to explain pleasantly and sensibly that if she didn't keep her mouth shut, they were not going to be able to hear anything that might be going on outside.

"You mean if she's trying to get in?" Jennifer flicked out the flashlight.

"No, Jennifer," he said carefully, wondering how anyone could be so dense. "I'm not talking about the cat."

"Well, Miss Gray *is* important."

"Not as important as my skin," he snorted, burrowing into his bed. "Now let's get some sleep.

I have a feeling we've got a long day ahead tomorrow."

And Blake was right.

Jennifer was up at the crack of dawn, still looking for the cat. "Here, kitty, kitty . . ." she called from the gallery above.

Bleary-eyed, he sat up and shook his head. She was unreal. Here they were, lost on an island—maybe being pursued this very minute—and she was worried about a silly cat! Blake crawled out of his sleeping bag and stretched in the brisk morning air. Even though the candy bars had been a godsend, his stomach still growled hungrily.

"Oh, you're up?" Jennifer called down.

"Yeah, thanks to you," he snorted, tying his shoes.

"We have to find her, Blake."

"And we also have to get out of here," he added, picking up a plank with a large nail protruding from its tip.

"What're you doing with that?"

"I'm going down to that kelp bed off shore and see if I can scrounge up a fish or two," he told her. "Maybe there are some oysters, too."

"Ugh."

"We'll need something that's going to stick to our ribs before we take off."

"Take off?" she questioned, leaning over the rail.

He nodded. "We can't hang around here much longer, Jennifer. It's the first place they're gonna come looking." Blake walked over to the knot hole and peered out. "But since you're up there, keep your eyes peeled, OK?"

"What do you think I've been doing?"

"I'm not talking about the cat," he said flatly, lifting the bolt and stepping into the foggy dawn.

Turning his thoughts toward the problem at hand, Blake hurried across the spit and down into the cove where the kelp bed drifted lazily off the rocks to his left. Although his makeshift spear was hardly the ideal way to catch bottom fish, he was thankful at least for the mist of fog that should provide a camouflage. But he knew he had to hurry. Once the fog lifted, Blake knew he would be a sitting duck.

Strings of seaweed and eelgrass clung to his shivering frame as he splashed and struggled in vain to spear a rockfish. Even the wheeling, whining gulls in the sky overhead seemed to be laughing at his stupid, futile efforts. Finally, he gave up and started back.

Grabbing a scrub juniper, Blake hoisted himself up the bank. Then suddenly, just before he reached the top, something instinctive told him to stop. To listen. *What is it? Voices? Or just the gulls?* His pulse quickened as he peered cautiously over the ridge.

And then he saw them in the distance. Two men with guns coming through the trees in the direction of the lighthouse. Hunters moving in for the kill. . . .

Gripped with sudden terror, Blake dropped like a boulder back onto the beach and raced toward the lighthouse. Fortunately the tide was out and although the jagged path of rocks was slippery and dangerous, he felt that he might be able to get to his sister without being seen by the men. But could he make it up that steep cliff just below the old sentinel? And could he reach her before they did?

In minutes, he was struggling up the treacherous wall of rock until at last, bleeding but safe, he had emerged directly behind the lighthouse. Breathing a quick prayer of thanks, Blake crawled like a weasel across the rocky ground, then climbed the back side of the old structure, easing his way through a rotting window frame in the tower. His heart was slamming hard like the surf below as he gazed down from the gallery.

The door was still bolted from the inside. He had made it! "Jennifer?" His raw whisper cut into the uncanny silence. "Jennifer, where are you?"

But there was no answer.

Blake tried to quiet the wild beating of his heart as he moved slowly, cautiously down the staircase. Where was his sister? Why didn't she answer?

"Jennifer. . . ."

Seven
The Hidden Pearl

"Hi!" Jennifer's slightly freckled nose poked up through a wide hole in the rotting floorboards beneath the stairway. "Guess what I found?"

Blake stared unbelievingly at the trapdoor and his sister who was motioning him excitedly down some kind of tunnel or underground passage.

"Come on." Her mop of brown hair disappeared below the floor. "You'll never believe it!"

She was right, he knew as he crawled down a shadowy earth-rock stepway and shut the door over his head. This was incredible! They were safe!

Jennifer was motioning him deeper into the passage with her flashlight. "Some discovery, huh?" she said excitedly.

"Shhh!" He froze, listening to a sudden muffled racket overhead. Was it their pursuers? Were they in the lighthouse now? "I . . . hear noises," he said quietly, his voice trembling.

"Yeah, well I did too." Her voice faded as she

led the way deeper into the eerie underground corridor. "Last night. I thought maybe I was dreaming or something."

"Last night?" He caught up with her and grabbed her arm. "You mean you heard the noises hours ago?"

She nodded.

"Why didn't you say something?" he whispered hoarsely, bracing himself against a rotting support that somehow managed to keep the earth and rock from caving in on them.

"You were acting like such a creep, I didn't think you cared what happened."

"What're you talking about?"

"This," she replied happily, turning and pointing her flashlight at a nest of dry earth. "And we thought she was just fat!"

Blake stared dumbfounded at the cat and four kittens.

"Aren't they the cutest little things?" Jennifer grinned, stroking the ecstatically happy new mother.

"I . . . I . . . Jennifer. . . ." Blake struggled to speak.

"Yeah?" She smiled up at him.

"I thought you were talking about those *men.*"

"What men?" She gulped.

"Those two men with guns," he said grimly, motioning toward the trapdoor above them.

The color drained from her face. "Oh, no!"

"I've been trying to tell you how serious this thing is, Jennifer, and it seems like all you've been worried about is that darned cat!"

"Well, I'll have you know that if it wasn't for

me and that cat, we'd probably still be up *there,"*
she said, pointing upward. "With them!"

Blake gave her a blank look, knowing she was
right. For a change, his sister was right.

"Are you sure you saw them coming toward the
lighthouse?" Jennifer edged closer. "With *guns?"*

He nodded in the shadows.

"What're we gonna do?" She gripped his arm
once more.

Blake wished he knew. Even if the men didn't
know about the tunnel, once they found the gear,
they would know someone was nearby. And then
they'd begin to search, wouldn't they? *It's just a
matter of time.*

"Well?" she prodded.

Blake took the flashlight from her quivering
hand and directed its beam deeper into the tunnel.
Webs, draped like Aunt Minnie's curtains, hung
everywhere.

"No," she said, shaking her head. "Let's not go
any farther."

"Why? You came this far."

"I know, but it was because I heard Miss Gray
and figured she was in trouble. I wasn't thinking
about spiderwebs and rats and stuff."

"And you don't think *we* might be in trouble if
they find that trapdoor?"

"Well, maybe they won't," she said hopefully. "I
mean, I wouldn't have found it if I hadn't heard
her meowing."

Blake went rigid.

"What's the matter?"

He backed up to the little earth-bed filled with
squirming bundles of gray fur. Miss Gray looked

up and meowed with delight. *"That's* what's the matter," he whispered gravely.

"Yeah, I see what you mean. She is kind of noisy, isn't she?" She wiped her sweaty hands off on the seat of her jeans.

"Whether we like it or not, I'm afraid we *have* to go deeper into the tunnel. And Miss Gray and the kittens are going with us." He tucked the kittens into a pouch he made with his baggy sweatshirt.

This time Jennifer didn't argue. She picked up the mother cat and followed him into the shadows.

With one hand Blake held the tiny balls of fur, and with the other he began knocking down spiders and cobwebs with his flashlight.

"Ugh!" Jennifer muttered from behind.

"Be thankful we found this tunnel," he snorted, brushing some broken glass aside with his shoe.

"We?" She stopped in her tracks.

Here we go again, Blake groaned. "Yeah, OK, Jennifer," he said, figuring it wasn't the time to get into another one of their stupid arguments again. He had a lot more important things on his mind right then, like—now where was this passage taking them? And was the air getting thinner, or was it just his imagination?

"Was this an old mine shaft or something?" she asked, breaking into his thoughts.

Blake kicked aside some more litter with his foot and paused. He had been wondering the same thing. And yet—if it was a mine shaft, why was it so cleverly hidden under the lighthouse? "I don't know," he said finally, kicking some more debris. "But somebody used this tunnel for something once." He shone his light at the glass and bones at his feet.

Bones? His heart almost stopped as he stared at the chalky white things lying everywhere. *What are bones doing in here?*

"What's the matter?" Jennifer nearly rammed into him.

"Oh, yeah, I . . . uh," he stammered. "I was . . . just thinking. . . ."

"About what?"

"Yeah, well I was thinking this probably isn't a mine shaft, Jennifer."

"Then what is it?" she asked, trying to calm the cat who was wriggling in her arms now.

"I'm . . . not sure."

"Well, me either," she said, backing up, "and I think Miss Gray feels the same way. Besides, we've gone far enough. They'll never hear any of us now."

Blake agreed and in a few moments had found another smooth nest of earth and rock. Carefully he placed the kittens against the soft fur of their mother, who was purring contentedly once more. "Now stay put," he said firmly, knowing cats sometimes did dumb things like drag their kittens back to the place where they had been born.

Suddenly he heard a strange sound. He stood up quickly and grabbed Jennifer's arm. "What's that?"

"It's my stomach," she said flatly. "I'm starving."

Relief washed over him like a wave. And he felt like laughing, except it wasn't funny. They *were* out of food and water.

"You didn't get a fish, huh?"

He shook his head in the shadows.

"Well, it wouldn't matter anyway," she said to him. "With somebody on our trail, we can't build a fire, and I'm *not* about to eat raw fish. Yuck."

He hoped it wouldn't come to that, but sooner or later they were going to have to do something. They had to eat. And they needed water. Soon.

Then Jennifer went rigid. "What's that?" she whispered. "I hear something. . . ."

Blake listened. He heard it too and this time it wasn't a growling stomach.

"Wh—what is it?" She was trembling like a jellyfish now.

The noise was coming from the unexplored end of the tunnel, and if Blake's heart would just quit pounding so loud, maybe he could hear. . . .

Eight
A Cave Grave

Petrified, Blake and Jennifer backed up slowly,
listening to the faint, ghostly wailing.

"Gulls, maybe?" Jennifer asked weakly.

"Gulls?" He kicked aside more glass and bones
in a nervous gesture. "What would sea gulls be
doing trapped in this tunnel? That's dumb."

"Maybe they're not trapped."

"Huh?"

"Maybe we're nearing the end of this thing," she
said bravely. "Maybe it ends at the water's edge."

A faint hope rose inside him. "You think so?"

She nudged him forward. "Let's find out."

They moved cautiously through the narrowing
snakelike passageway, listening to the cries grow
louder as the pungent smell of salt became
stronger. And when Blake finally saw the faint
speck of blue in the distance, he almost exploded
with joy.

In a few moments they had reached the patch of
blue and the tunnel's outlet.

"I just can't believe it!" Jennifer threw up her

hands and started laughing as she gazed around at the familiar glazed walls of the cave where they had spent their first night. "So this is where the tunnel ends!"

Blake shook his head in amazement, listening to the wailing gulls in the sky beyond. "Crazy birds!" he laughed. "Crazy everything!"

"And we thought we were trapped in this place that first night," she went on, "when all the time we could have gone to the lighthouse by way of the tunnel!"

He nodded, still shaking his head in disbelief. "Some discovery, huh?"

"Yeah," he said carefully, "and I hope we're the only ones who have made it."

"What are you saying?"

Blake glanced back over his shoulder into the dark corridor behind them. "I'm saying, I hope it's only you and me and Miss Gray who know about this secret."

"Oh, yeah," she agreed quickly. "I see what you mean. Maybe we'd better leave, huh?" She leaned out and looked on the wet rocks below. "The tide's right."

"And go where?" Blake asked.

"I'm not sure. Anywhere but here, I guess," she replied nervously. "Anyhow, I hate caves. Besides, what if they're coming down that tunnel *right this minute?*"

"But what if they aren't, Jennifer? Can't you see we may have found the perfect hiding place?"

Jennifer wasn't convinced.

"And," he went on, "if they haven't found that trapdoor, they're going to be searching every square inch of land around here. They might even be directly over our heads on the bluff right now," he said, pulling her away from the ledge where her sweatshirt flapped in the warm breeze.

"But, how can we *know?*" she asked worriedly. "And what about later on, if they do find the trapdoor? They could sneak up from behind when we're sleeping or not looking."

Blake thought for a moment, then glanced around at the broken glass on the cave floor. "Sure," his voice rose. "That's it!"

"What's it?" She edged closer.

"We'll set up a warning signal," he told her. "These old broken bottles might be good for something after all."

She stared at the broken glass littering the rock floor. "Somebody sure drank a lot of pop or something, huh?"

"Uh, it wasn't pop, Jennifer."

"It wasn't?"

Blake shook his head. "Not quite."

"You mean whiskey and stuff like that?"

"Rum is more like it," he replied, crouching down and picking up a piece of glass with a time-etched label. It was all beginning to come together in his head now: the tunnel hidden so well under the lighthouse, leading to the cave and then to the open strait. . . .

"What're you getting at?" she prodded.

"I'm saying that I'll bet anything this cave and tunnel---maybe even the lighthouse---were used by rumrunners a long time ago.

"What kind of runners?" She wrinkled her nose in puzzlement.

"People and boats that once used to bring rum and other booze back and forth across borders illegally. Haven't you ever heard about Prohibition, Jennifer?"

"You mean a long time ago when it was against the law to sell beer and stuff?"

He nodded and brushed aside a few bones with his shoe, hoping she hadn't noticed. It was all beginning to make sense. Had this cave been a graveyard, too? Salty Bob had told him about all the smuggling that used to go on in the islands, and it hadn't been just booze and drugs, either. The old-timer had told Blake about foreigners who had been smuggled in on ships and whose lives were of no more value than a few dollars in a game of poker.

"What's this cave got to do with all that?" Jennifer broke into his thoughts.

Blake turned to her. "A lot of the islands were used for smuggling," he told her. "Salty Bob said that bootlegging was big business once. Big money. And what better place to move illegal contraband than isolated islands without border stations? What a set-up, Jennifer. Boats moving in and out, and nobody knowing if they were carrying salmon or crab or what."

"That's happening again, isn't it? Back in that meadow."

He nodded. "That green gold back there is becoming one of the biggest moneymaking crops in the country and I'll bet that field we found is probably worth more than a million bucks to those guys, too."

"No kidding?"

"Yeah, so maybe we'd better get this warning thing set up," he replied.

"What's the plan?"

"A glass barricade," he explained. "Collect all the broken glass you can."

Without protest, Jennifer began gathering up the bits and pieces of glass lying everywhere. "What are these?" she asked absently, showing him some chalky white things she'd found.

Blake bit his lip. He was afraid she was going to make the discovery sooner or later. "Uh, maybe fish bones," he said casually.

She tipped her head questioningly. "Aren't they a little bit big for that?"

"Ever hear of whales, Jennifer?" he laughed stiffly, hoping to divert her mind from the very real possibility that she might be holding fragments of a human skeleton.

She shrugged and went on gathering up the glass pieces, mumbling something about wondering how a whale got into the cave.

Fortunately she didn't bring it up again, and Blake was glad. It was just one more thing she didn't need to be worrying about. They had enough problems already.

Before long, they had collected enough glass for the barricade. Blake slipped off his jacket and after they had filled it with the glass, carried it back into the tunnel.

"I think this is far enough," he said finally, shining his flashlight around in the narrow section of the corridor. Carefully, quietly, they set the jacket-pouch down and began to construct the nearly invisible shelf of glass which spanned the width of the passageway.

"You can barely see it," Jennifer said with satisfaction when they had finished. "It looks like part of the floor, doesn't it?"

"Yeah, except when they walk into it, they'll know it isn't," he added ruefully. "And so will we."

"Then we take off?" she asked.

He nodded and led the way back to the cave.

"But what if the tide's in?" she went on, walking over to the yawning mouth of the cave and glancing down at the wet rocks below.

"Then we've got a problem," he said. "A *big* problem."

Jennifer swallowed hard and turned to her brother. "Yeah, and with our luck. . . ."

"It hasn't been just luck, Jennifer."

She nodded. "I guess you're right, but I'm still sorta scared, aren't you?"

"Yeah, a little," he admitted.

And hungry," she added. "Starving, as a matter of fact. What're we gonna do, Blake?"

"If all goes well, I may try for some fish after dark," he said, gazing down at the tide moving in.

"What good would that do? It's not safe to build a fire and cook it."

"It might come to where that's not going to matter, Jennifer."

"Oh, no!" She shook her head with determination. "No raw fish for me! No way. . . ."

"Maybe we won't have that choice."

"I am *not* interested in throwing up, thank you."

68

"Then you're not starving," he said flatly, ending the discussion. *But it might come to that,* he thought grimly. He had to get some fish—oysters—something.

They were silent after that. Waiting. Listening. Wondering what they were going to do next. And when the sun finally dropped on the western horizon and darkness fell, Blake knew they had one more problem. Without their sleeping bags, they were going to be cold. Very, very cold. Already he felt the chill coming in off the strait.

Finally he got up and motioned for Jennifer to follow him deeper into the tunnel. "We'd better get out of the wind for the night. It might be a little warmer back in here."

"Sleep back in *there?* No!" She bristled, staring warily into the snake of darkness. "I'm not—"

"Jennifer," he said sharply, trying to keep control. "Will you please keep your voice down? They might be on that bluff above us right now."

"So . . . so what?" Her voice shivered in the rising wind as she wrapped her arms tighter around her tense frame. "We're just a couple of kids messing around, and I dropped my canteen. What's the big deal, anyway? We can tell them we think their maple trees are pretty."

He shook his head hopelessly, then turned and walked into the tunnel.

Reluctantly she followed him, still rattling on like a nervous woodpecker. "I have a feeling this is going to be another terrible night," she said when they had finally curled up into a fairly sheltered niche of earth and rock. "Terrible."

Blake feared she might be right, and somewhere

between midnight and morning, his worst fears became reality.

"What's that?" Jennifer woke up instantly to the sound of falling glass.

Blake went rigid. He couldn't answer. But he didn't have to, because he already knew. They both knew.

Someone was coming. . . .

Nine
Unhinged

Terrified, they leaped up and raced toward the mouth of the cave where the moon, though partially hidden by clouds, cast a faint light on the surf below.

"Oh, no!" Jennifer cried, staring down. "The tide's in! We're trapped!"

Blake's mind reeled. He knew that if they tried to swim, they would never make it. The undertow would carry them to the same seaweed grave that had swallowed their boat. *What should we do?* he wondered wildly.

"Meow."

"Jennifer, this isn't the time. . . ." He whirled around angrily.

"But, Blake!" she sputtered. "It's only Miss Gray!"

Dizzy with relief, he stared dumbfounded at the cat. *That crazy cat!*

"Miss Gray!" Jennifer exploded into giggles as she picked up the vibrating ball of fur. "You sure had us worried!"

Blake rolled his eyes and sighed in a mixture of relief and exasperation.

"But we're glad it's you," Jennifer went on. "Oh, wow! Are we glad it's you!"

Blake turned and hurried back toward the barricade.

"I'll bet she was just hungry," Jennifer rattled on, following him.

"Well, she's not gonna find anything down here," he muttered, kneeling down beside the flattened wall of glass and examining it with his flashlight.

"Maybe when she finds that out, she'll give up," Jennifer suggested, rubbing her sleepy eyes.

"Yeah, and go somewhere else," Blake turned and held her gaze in the shadows.

"Huh?" She cocked her head curiously.

"She'll go back to the lighthouse. There's plenty of food running around up there."

"But, we shut the trapdoor!"

"Jennifer," he sighed. "How did she get into the tunnel to have those kittens in the first place?"

"Oh, yeah." Jennifer understood. "I guess squeezing through a hole or a crack in the floor is nothing for a cat, is it?"

Blake nodded. "And," he went on evenly, "if those men *are* up there, she's likely to lead them straight to our hiding place."

"But maybe they aren't up there," she smiled hopefully, still clinging to the cat. "We don't know that *for sure,* do we?"

"No," he replied carefully. "And there's only one way to find out."

"Oh, no!" She drew back, shaking her head firmly.

"Look, Jennifer, we need our gear. There's still some water in that canteen and without it and the rest of our stuff—"

"But they might be watching for us," she cut in.

"Maybe, but my guess is that if they *are* up in that lighthouse, they're probably sleeping right now. I can just sneak through the trapdoor and get our things and then we can hide out here until we figure out what to do next."

She groaned. "Can't we think of someplace else to hide? I *hate* it in here."

"We're a lot safer here than out there, Jennifer," he reminded her. "And I'm not just thinking of those men, either."

"Yeah, I know," she said darkly. "The grizzly."

Blake got up and started back into the passageway. "Keep the cat here, and I'll be back as soon as I can," he said, disappearing into the darkness. Blake's knuckles whitened as he gripped the flashlight tighter and moved cautiously up the earth-rock tunnel toward the lighthouse. The minutes seemed like hours until, at last, he reached the rock steps that led to the trapdoor just over his head. His knees felt like jellyfish as he flicked out his flashlight and moved upward in the smothering darkness, groping for the rough surface with his hand. Drawing a quick breath, he lifted the splintered boards and peered cautiously around in the pale light shed by the moon slipping down from the gallery.

He sighed thankfully when he saw that

everything was exactly as he and Jennifer had left it. Except for one thing. The door was hanging half off its hinges—creaking like a ghostly apparition in the wind. Blake felt a chill. *So they have been here,* he said to himself, grabbing their gear and making a quick retreat back into the underground corridor. Fortunately, there were still some berries left in the can which should stave off their near-starvation a little longer. But how much longer could they hold out? And how much longer before the men returned?

Jennifer was overjoyed to see him. "I thought you'd never get back!" she cried, reaching for her sleeping bag and wrapping it around her shivering frame.

"They aren't there," Blake said, handing her the can of berries.

"Thank goodness for that," she replied, collapsing on the floor and beginning to fill her mouth with the sweet fruit.

"But they were," he went on, sitting down beside her. "They almost ripped the door off the hinges." Uncapping the canteen, he drank thirstily, then handed it to his sister.

"They . . . were . . . there?" she nearly choked on her mouthful of berries.

He nodded soberly.

Miss Gray joined them, but except for a little water they shared with her, she was hardly enthusiastic. Berries held no lure for the plump mother cat who seemed to have no shortage of food supply. Before long, she had disappeared.

"I'll bet she went back to her kittens," Jennifer remarked, wiping some red juice off her chin.

"Or the lighthouse," Blake added, helping himself to the remaining berries. "Should be plenty of dinner running around up there."

"Ugh," Jennifer grimaced. "And you're *sure* no one was up there?"

"Not right now, but my guess is they'll be back."

She shivered in the chill. "What'll we do? We can't just stay and rot in this cave."

"I know," he agreed. "I've spent half the night thinking about it, and the only thing I can come up with is making a getaway on their boat."

"Their boat?" She faced him in astonishment. He nodded.

"But there wasn't any boat. . . ."

"We didn't see one, Jennifer, but there has to be something moving that crop and those men on and off this island. Sooner or later there'll be a boat in that cove. We just have to wait, that's all."

"But isn't that a bit risky?" she said thickly. "I mean, how are we going to take a bunch of criminals?"

"By using our heads and remembering we've got more than just luck with us," he answered.

Jennifer wrapped the sleeping bag tighter around her shoulders and nodded. She understood.

Finally a gray dawn filtered into the cave.

Jennifer got up and walked over to the opening of the cave and stared at the blanket of fog hovering over the strait. "I haven't seen a boat in these waters anywhere," she said despairingly. "It's like we're in a wilderness. Somewhere beyond nowhere."

"We are, Jennifer. And that's why it's such an

ideal place for those pot farmers."

"And because of that grizzly, even the government is helping keep people away," she added grimly. "If they only knew what they were protecting!"

Blake stared at the endless haze of gray and nodded.

"At least with our gear gone, maybe those men will figure we left the lighthouse. And the island."

"With what?" he asked flatly. "Wings?"

"Well, it might throw 'em off," she went on, taking one long, last drink from his canteen. "At least until we can find the boat. Or something."

He stared at the outgoing tide, hoping she was right. But one thing he knew for sure was that they had better scrounge up some food before they made the next move.

"What're you thinking?" She broke into his thoughts.

"I'm thinking we've got to eat."

"We just did. The berries."

"No, I mean more than just berries. We have to have something that's going to stick to our ribs before we—"

"But we can't build a fire," she interrupted too quickly, "and I already told you that I *can't* eat raw fish. . . ."

"I know."

"Then, what're you getting at?"

"Limpets."

"What?" she exploded, nearly falling over backward. "You mean those slimy little Chinamen's hats sticking to those rocks down there?" She was pointing down in disgust.

"Yeah, Jennifer," he sighed.

"Not *me!*" She backed up, shaking her tousled head of long hair firmly. "No way!"

Blake threw up his hands. "We might just *have* to, Jennifer. Anyway, Uncle Jack eats 'em all the time. Raw clams, too."

"I know—and it makes me sick just thinking about it."

"You're gonna be a lot sicker if all you eat are berries."

"Yeah, well, I'll take my chances, thanks," she said acidly.

Blake dropped the subject since he didn't feel like having a full-scale war right then. For the time being, berries would just have to suffice. Besides, he knew they needed water. But if they were going back to the meadow, they'd have to hurry. Once the fog lifted, they'd be easy prey. Blake sensed that he and his sister were in a lot more danger than either one of them dared admit. A million-dollar smuggling operation was nothing to mess with. And neither was a renegade grizzly.

He explained the plan.

"You mean, if something goes wrong, we make tracks for the lighthouse, right?"

"Right," he said, hooking the canteen onto his belt and handing her the empty can for more berries.

"But what if they see us?" she asked, following him down onto the rocks. "What if they find the trapdoor and try to follow us?"

"By that time, we'll be on our way."

"On our way?" Her voice quivered in the wind. "On our way where?"

"God only knows," he said, moving surefootedly along the wet rocks toward the cove. *He's the only one who really knows.*

"Yeah. Well, maybe you're right, but I sure wish he'd clue us in, too. I mean, this whole thing is like a big dumb puzzle that doesn't fit together."

Blake agreed. Something was missing. A clue that was eluding him—dangling like fish bait in his mind.

What was it?

Ten
A Grizzly Dilemma

Blake left Jennifer picking berries and went down to the creek to get some water. He had just finished filling his canteen when he heard the voices. *The men.*

He froze, knowing it was too late to warn her. *Will she hear them?* he wondered frantically, ducking behind the upturned root of a fallen tree. *Will she remember to run for the lighthouse?*

"Just a matter of time," a crude, sneering voice cut into Blake's wild thoughts. Blake's skin crawled as he watched the two men with rifles appear in the thicket. The huge bearded one with the evil voice was still laughing. It was hard to see clearly, but from a distance the other man appeared bald, except for a few straggles of yellow hair dangling like wet sea grass. He reminded Blake of a bony heron.

"Been needin' a little compost anyhow, eh, Grizzly?" the birdlike man said in a mocking jeer.

Grizzly? Blake caught his breath and ducked

farther behind the root wad, watching the men move stealthily through the underbrush toward his sister. *He called him . . . Grizzly!*

What should I do next? he wondered frantically as he tried to stop the wild hammering inside his chest. Now that the fog had lifted, Blake knew that if he tried to reach Jennifer first, they would both be caught. Those were high-powered rifles the men were carrying, and Blake sensed they would not hesitate to use them.

His wild thoughts raced like his pulse as he followed the men through the tangle of vines. And then he saw her. She was racing like a sandpiper through the meadow toward the lighthouse.

And the men were close on her heels. Laughing. Stalking, like wild animals. They had seen her disappear into the lighthouse. They had trapped their little bird. . . .

Hurry, Jennifer! Blake cried silently, frantically. *The trapdoor Quick!*

Then, as soon as the men had disappeared into the lighthouse behind her, he cut across the spit and raced down the bank into the cove. Rocks flew and salt grass stung his cheeks and arms as he ran toward the cave, leaping over boulders and driftwood, yet still keeping close to the low, overhanging protection of the cliff.

At last he could see the cave's mouth. *What now?* he wondered nervously, glancing back at the steadily encroaching tide. In minutes they would be trapped. . . .

"Blake?" Jennifer's breathless voice knifed through his frenzied thoughts.

He whirled around and stared up at the wide

brown eyes peering down at him and heaved a huge sigh of relief. "Did they see you?" he cried, beckoning her down with a trembling hand. "I mean . . . the trapdoor?"

"I don't think so," she sputtered, clawing her way down the ragged rock wall. "But, they saw me go in that lighthouse and they're gonna wonder how I disappeared so fast. They'll be looking. . . ."

"Yeah," Blake said, motioning quickly for her to follow him back to the cove. The water was ankle-deep now.

"But if they're in the lighthouse, they'll see us!"

She drew back, trying to keep her balance as the sucking tide encroached. "They can see everything from that tower! Everything!"

"*If* they're still in the lighthouse."

"You mean maybe they're not?" She froze. "Maybe . . . maybe they're in the tunnel . . . right this . . . minute?"

He nodded gravely and took off running.

She followed him in a wild race against time. Dirt and rocks flew up and stung them like hornets as they ran across the cove and up the bank into the trees.

"Where're we going?" Jennifer gasped, wiping her sweaty face with the torn sleeve of her shirt.

"That dock," he called back. "Maybe we'll find their boat! Hurry!"

But when they reached the old boat landing at last, their hopes were dashed. Except for the lone warning sign, the shoreline and cove were deserted.

"There's no boat," she cried, struggling against tears.

"Maybe they've got it hidden," he said, gazing around. "Maybe they know the government might get suspicious and check if they see a boat hanging around." Blake brushed aside a coil of rope that was draped over the sign and read it once more. "Nobody's supposed to be trespassing on this island, remember?"

She sighed, then turned and hurried down into the cove past the ramshackle dock that was quaking in the gentle waves.

Blake was still staring at the sign when she called up to him. "What's the matter?"

He wasn't sure, but he felt vaguely uneasy about something. But what?

"Come on!" she called, cutting into his disquieting thoughts. "If we're going to find that boat, we'd better do it before dark!"

They leaped over rocks and logs and tidepools, scouring every nook and cranny of the shoreline south of the boat dock, but the search yielded nothing. There was no boat anywhere around.

Discouraged, Jennifer collapsed on a log. "I just don't understand. If there isn't a boat, then how did those men get here? And how can they smuggle their stuff off this island?"

Blake stood on the shore of the small, well-hidden saltwater lagoon, his hair ruffling in the rising breeze. "Maybe it's because the boat only comes to the island now and then," he replied.

Her troubled eyes searched his face questioningly.

"And if it does," he went on, "I don't think we'd see it."

"Why's that?"

"Because it probably comes only at night, when it won't be seen," he told her.

Jennifer wrapped her arms around herself and shivered in the cooling wind coming off the water.

"But I think we're safe here," he said carefully, glancing around at the camouflage of trees encircling the tiny lagoon.

"Well, *I* sure don't feel very safe," she shot back, her eyes glancing furtively around. "Those horrible men might be tracking us down right this minute! And besides, what about the grizzly? You said he was probably on the other end of the island and I'll bet that's where we are right now!" Her chin quivered.

Blake started to speak, but before he could get the words out, she had burst into tears.

"And it's our own fault!" she wailed.

"Our fault?" He faced her in astonishment. "How can you say that?"

"We haven't prayed!"

"Jennifer," he said, shaking his head incredulously, "we've hardly had any time to pray!"

"That's no excuse."

"Excuse?" He was still shaking his head. "For Pete's sake, who needs an excuse? What we've needed is help. And we've gotten it," he told her. "Why do you think we're still alive?"

"But, I'm scared." She sniffed, wiping her eyes.

Blake shrugged absently. "Well, maybe I am, too. But that doesn't mean God has deserted us."

"But, if we don't even ask. . . ."

"Look, Jennifer," he cut in, "if everything depended on what we did or didn't do, we'd be in worse shape than that dead rat Miss Gray was hauling around. That's why we need Him so much, Jen. That's one of the reasons I gave my life to Him."

"But, we're *supposed* to pray," she went on, her expression still as troubled as the clouding sky.

"Sure, but maybe just saying 'thanks' a little bit more often is the best kind of prayer we can ever have."

Even though she made no reply, Blake sensed that she understood. And even though the air and sky around them were growing strangely dark and troubled, he felt better. A lot better.

"Sometimes just saying things out loud helps," he said finally, "especially when your insides feel knotted up like a bunch of rope."

She faced him suddenly.

"What's the matter?"

"Knots. Rope." She leaped up. "That gives me an idea!"

He made a face in the haze of dusk. "What're you talking about?"

"A raft," she said, pointing excitedly to the logs lying scattered around. "We can rope some driftwood together and make a raft!"

"There isn't any rope."

"Not here, but there is some back by that dock. Remember?"

Blake's mind backed up, remembering the coil draped on the warning sign.

"Why not sneak back and get it?" she went on eagerly.

"Isn't that a bit risky, Jennifer?"

"You think messing around with two men, two guns, and a grizzly bear *isn't?*"

84

He gave her a blank look.

"So you'd better hurry!" his sister went on, giving him a quick shove.

"Me?" He nearly fell off the log. "What do you mean, *me?"*

She gave him a shocked look. "You mean, you're scared? After all you just said. . . ."

"Look Jennifer," he snorted, "if I wasn't a little bit scared, I'd probably be up on some cloud right now playing a guitar."

"Harp," she corrected.

Blake rolled his eyes and got up. "Yeah, harping is more like it," he agreed, walking off.

"I'll get the driftwood," she said helpfully, waving him off.

"Sure." He paused and turned to her. "But be careful."

She caught her breath and nodded bravely.

"You might get a sliver," he said.

Eleven
Daft Raft

By the time Blake got back with the rope, the tide had nearly pinned Jennifer against the cliff. She was struggling to keep the wood she had gathered from floating away. "I thought you'd never get back," she cried, shivering.

Blake crouched down and examined the small heap of lumber she had gathered.

"You didn't see anything, huh?" she questioned.

He shook his head, dragging the logs higher onto what was left of the small beach.

"Maybe those men didn't even find that trap-door." She smiled stiffly. "Maybe they're still waiting for us to come back to the lighthouse!"

"Maybe," he said carefully, uncoiling the rope.

"If it wasn't for that grizzly, I'd almost feel safe for the night," she went on.

"Jennifer," Blake said slowly, "I think our grizzly has two feet. Not four."

"Huh?" She caught his anxious gaze.

He went on, "I knew something didn't fit and then, all of a sudden, it hit my mind."

"What . . . hit your mind?"

"The guy with the chicken legs called the bushy-faced one Grizzly."

She swallowed hard. "Wh . . . what's that got to do with it?"

"He even looked like a grizzly, Jennifer. Jagged yellow teeth, everything."

She paled in the half-light of approaching darkness.

"And then I started thinking about those puny little signs the government supposedly posted," he continued. "And I knew."

"You knew *what?*"

"I knew why we hadn't seen any bear signs on this island. No slashes on the tree bark. Nothing."

"But the trap," she reminded him.

"That trap wasn't for a grizzly, Jennifer."

She gasped.

Blake held his voice steady and went on to explain. "Those signs were put there to keep people off the island."

Jennifer shook her head, confused.

"And they're small enough so that they can't be spotted by a Coast Guard vessel cruising by. It's a perfect camouflage."

She was shaking her head in amazement. "And it worked until we came along and fouled things up. Right?"

"Right," Blake said. "That's why we're leaving tonight."

"Tonight?" She reeled around and glanced at the troubled water and sky. "But we can't! It's almost dark, and anyway—a storm is blowing up! Just look!" she said, pointing to the whitecaps lashing out like ghostly tongues against a shroud of threatening sky.

"I know, but what kind of chance do you think we'd have against those rifles in broad daylight, Jennifer?"

"But the tides!" she countered. "They're too strong!"

"A strong current may be our only chance of getting out of here," he said, beginning to rope the logs together. "Now, try to find something we can use for paddles while I finish this."

"But what about Miss Gray?"

"Miss Gray?" He glanced up in astonishment. "What's Miss Gray got to do with it?"

"I'm worried about her and the kittens. They might not survive."

Blake could hardly believe his ears. "Jennifer," he said sharply, "if you don't hurry up and find some paddles, *we* might not either! Now, move!"

She was still mumbling something about Miss Gray being more important than he realized when she returned with two flat boards.

"Good," Blake glanced up, securing the last knot in the makeshift craft. "Now help me," he said, shoving the clumsy thing into the water. "The tide's changing!"

In seconds the raft was afloat.

"Jump!" he ordered, tossing the makeshift paddles onto the lashed wood, which was beginning to roll like a package of wieners in a simmering pot.

"Ugh! This is terrible!" Jennifer groaned, leaping

on and grabbing the center rope to keep her balance.

Blake gave the raft one last push, then jumped on. "Whose idea was it?"

"Well . . . I changed my mind!" she cried. "We'll never make it!"

"Yes we will," he said firmly, handing her a paddle and hoping the tide would continue to cooperate and keep moving them away from the island, so that by dawn they would be well out of range of those guns. "Now row, Jennifer! Row like crazy!"

The ominous sky grew blacker as the feeble craft moved with the tide, bobbing and swirling like aimless debris on the dark water.

"Where's the moon?" Jennifer sputtered, trying to stay upright and paddle at the same time. "I can't even see!"

"That's good," he said, trying to hold down the foreboding in his voice. "It means . . . we can't . . . be seen, either."

Jennifer swallowed hard, still struggling against the rising wind and surf. Overhead, storm clouds hung threateningly in the heavy, troubled sky. "But it's so cold!" She was trying to maintain control. "And we don't even have our jackets, Blake. Our sleeping bags and everything are in the cave. We'll freeze to death out here!"

He knew she might be right as he struggled on through the unfamiliar waters. But they had to hold on. They had to keep on believing they would make it no matter how great the odds were against them. He knew they couldn't give up now.

And then Blake saw a light in the distance. "Hold it!" he said to his sister.

Jennifer whirled around, the wind slapping her hair and clothing like wet seaweed.

"Huh? What is it?"

"Yes. . . ." Blake's voice trembled as he gripped the center rope and steadied himself. "It *is* a light, Jennifer. A boat!"

"Oh, thank heavens!" she cried out. "We're—"

"Shhh!" he ordered.

"Wh . . . why?"

"Because it might be *theirs!*"

Her brown eyes widened as she stared at the light moving closer. "You mean those smugglers?"

He nodded. "I have a feeling we've drifted into that darned cove."

"You mean by the old dock?"

"Yeah," he whispered hoarsely, "and I'll bet anything they're making connections tonight, too."

Jennifer tried to speak, but no words came. She could scarcely move.

"So let's get out of here as fast as we can," Blake said carefully, trying to paddle backward now. But the pull of the tide was too strong. The raft only turned in circles.

"We'll never make it!" Jennifer wailed, fighting against the stubborn current and her tears. "That boat is coming too close! Oh, Blake. . . ."

Then, suddenly, the oncoming lights from the high bow turned and moved toward shore.

Jennifer gasped with relief. "Oh, thank—"

"Shhh!" Blake commanded as the little raft

heaved awkwardly in the wake of the huge boat. "They're still too close. Don't talk. Don't even move."

"How can I help it?" she moaned. "I'm bobbing like a cork on this stupid thing and, besides that, I feel like throwing up!"

"Don't you dare!" He glared.

Thankfully, the lights faded into the darkness of the cove.

"They didn't see us, did they?" Jennifer whispered.

"No." He wiped the sweat and spray from his face. "But I saw their boat, and it was a seiner, Jennifer. A purse seiner."

"Oh, thank heavens!" She nearly fell over backward with joy. "I thought it was the smugglers' boat!"

He faced her in astonishment. "It *is.*"

"But you just said it was a fishing boat. . . ."

Blake shook his head in the spray-fogged darkness, wondering how anybody could be so dense. "What do you think pot smugglers are gonna do, Jennifer? Paint *Marijuana Baby* on a fancy rig and cruise around in broad daylight?"

A sheet of salt spray whipped against her, nearly throwing her off the raft. "Forget it," she choked, regaining her balance. "Just forget it."

Blake figured he would do just that. There were a lot more important things to face right then anyway, he knew as he listened to the warning clang of a bell buoy somewhere in the distance grow louder and louder. And when the first drop of rain hit his face, his worst fears were confirmed. A full-fledged storm was upon them. His knuckles

92

whitened as he clung tighter to the center rope. The raft was heaving dangerously now, but at least it was moving away from the cove.

"This tide . . . this storm. . . ." Jennifer's faltering voice cut into his troubled thoughts. "Where's it taking us?"

Blake faced the bleak horizon. If only he knew. . . .

Twelve
Reluctant Return

The wind bit with icy teeth as the desperate pair fought against the sudden, frenzied storm and struggled to stay afloat. Angry waves chopped and chewed at the raft until, after what seemed like an eternity, they hit a reef.

Jennifer screamed as the raft shattered like kindling on the rocks. Making a wild grab for his sister, Blake leaped blindly into the darkness, groping for solid footing.

"No. . . ." Jennifer was spitting salt water and clawing like a crazed animal. "Help! Help!"

"Cut it out!" Blake spat out the words as soon as he caught his breath. "I . . . I think we're back where we started!"

"The lagoon?" she sputtered, clinging to a slimy rock.

"No, the cave. Near the lighthouse," he said breathlessly.

"Oh, no!" she wailed. "Octopuses. . . ."

"Shhh!" Blake said sharply, gripping her arm. "They might be waiting!"

"Help!" She screamed louder, clawing and groping wildly. "Octopuses . . . help!"

"I'm talking about those *men,* Jennifer." He shook her trembling frame, trying to silence her. "Now, be quiet. They could be in the lighthouse! Let's go."

She fell suddenly silent, following his lead along the familiar rocky spit toward the base of the cliff. "But they *can* pull you under," she muttered grimly as she clawed her way up the wall of rock and into the cave. "They squeeze you to death with those horrible tentacles and. . . ."

But Blake was no longer listening. He had already disappeared into the tunnel.

"Hey, wait a minute!" she cried. "Where are you going?" The wind off the water was whipping her wet clothing against her shivering frame.

"To see if our sleeping bags and stuff are still back here," her brother called back, his teeth chattering with cold.

"Why wouldn't they be?" she asked, catching up with him.

Blake hesitated, then spoke. "If the men found the tunnel. . . ." He didn't finish.

"Oh, yeah," she said tightly, following him into the passage where every breath, every footstep echoed. "I . . . see what you mean."

But when he stumbled into the gear, he almost exploded with joy. Blake grabbed his warm, dry sleeping bag and began hugging it like a baby. Everything was still upside down and crazy, but they were still alive. And Blake knew why. "Thanks," he said under his breath once more. "Thanks a lot."

"Huh?" Jennifer gave him a blank look as she peeled off her wet outer clothing and crawled into her sleeping bag. "Yeah, well, you're welcome."

"Jennifer. . . ."

"Wait a minute." She sat up in the darkness. "Thanks for what?"

Blake broke out laughing. "Forget it," he said finally, figuring he'd try to explain later. Right now they were safe and that was all that mattered. "Let's get some sleep now, OK?" He was still smiling as he curled up like a coon in a burrow.

"Sleep?" she said in disbelief. "Are you kidding, Blake?"

"Jennifer. . . ."

"How are we supposed to sleep with *them* waiting for us at the other end of the tunnel? Waiting to trap us like rats? Maybe they're coming down the passage right this minute," she went on, her voice rising. "Maybe we'll be dead—"

"Jennifer," he said acidly, poking his nose out of his sleeping bag, "will you be quiet long enough for me to tell you something?"

"Yeah?"

"Once I started thinking about it, I realized those guys probably aren't in the lighthouse. I'll bet anything they're back at that dock with the boat, loading the grass."

"Loading the *grass?*"

"Yeah," he replied. "So let's get some sleep. We're going to need all the strength we can get to face what's ahead."

"Well, that sure doesn't make any sense," she muttered, burrowing back down into her bed.

"What doesn't?"

"How come they're loading grass onto the boat? I thought it was a dope ring."

Blake couldn't believe what he was hearing. How could anybody be so dumb! "Jennifer," he said flatly, "sometimes marijuana is called grass."

"That's stupid," she said, pulling the sleeping bag over her head. "That's *really* stupid!"

Thankfully, she didn't say anything after that, and the next thing Blake knew, it was morning. He was awakened by the sound of wailing gulls circling a dead crab in the rocks just below the cave.

"So, now what?" Jennifer asked, poking her nose out from her warm nest.

Blake got up and stretched his stiff joints in the cool air. "I'm not sure," he replied, slipping on his heavy shirt and walking over to the mouth of the cave. "At least the storm is over, though."

"I'm still worried."

"Yeah, well so am I," he replied, agreeing with her for a change.

"If she was still in the tunnel, she would have come to us last night, don't you think?"

"Huh?"

"Miss Gray." Jennifer walked up to him and sighed. "She would have been here by now unless something was wrong. Maybe the kittens are sick or—"

"Jennifer!" Blake was shaking his head in complete amazement. "I can't believe this!"

"What'll we do?" she went on in earnest.

"We'll try to get off the island. That's what we'll do!"

"But what about Miss Gray and the kittens?"

Her brow was creased with a worried frown as she zipped up her hooded sweatshirt.

"Miss Pearl Gray and her kittens will be fine, Jennifer. It's *us* I'm thinking about."

"You're cruel, Blake. Heartless."

"Yeah, and I'm also still alive," he said dryly, crawling out of the cave. "Which is the way I intend to keep it," he added.

"Where're you going?"

"To check the shoreline and see if any of that rope or lumber washed back up last night," he called up. But if he was going to attempt another raft, he would have to hurry. It was only a matter of time before the men might return.

Jennifer shrugged and picked up the flashlight, turning and heading in the opposite direction. "Here kitty, kitty, kitty," she called bravely, moving into the darkness of the tunnel. "Miss Gray, where are you?"

A warming sun gradually broke through the clouds as Blake scoured the beach, searching for remnants of the raft. But his search proved fruitless. Not even a shred of rope lay on the wet rocks that were beginning to steam in the early-morning sun.

Discouraged, he sat down on a flat rock and stared blankly at the blurred horizon. "Why? I just don't understand. . . ."

And then he saw it.

It was only a speck in the distance, but he knew it was a boat. Except for the smugglers' seiner, it was the first one he had seen since they washed up on this island. He strained against the glare of sun, and his heart fell. The vessel seemed to be

99

moving due west. It wasn't even coming their way!

"No!" he cried angrily, reeling around and racing up into the cave to find his sister. "Jennifer! A boat! We've gotta signal! Jennifer. . . ."

But when he reached the cave, he found that his sister was nowhere around. *Jennifer, if you're chasing that darned cat again, I'll . . . I'll. . . .*

Frantic, he gazed around, then grabbed a shirt from his pack and ran back down to the rocks. "Here!" he cried out, waving the dirty white flag-shirt wildly. "We're here! See? Don't you see us?"

But he knew no one on the vessel had seen him. The boat continued on its westward course while he yelled and waved and cried out in vain. Hope oozed out of him as he turned and walked back to the cave, the shirt-flag hanging limp and useless in his hand.

"It's too late. Too late. . . ."

Thirteen
Crazy Contraband

"Blake . . . Blake . . . Blake. . . ."

He was leaning against the ragged mouth of the cave when he heard his sister's voice echoing from the tunnel. *It's too late, Jennifer,* he said silently. Angrily. *If you'd just been here when I needed you. If you hadn't been chasing that dumb cat. . . .*

"Blake!" Jennifer was suddenly beside him, clutching her sleeping bag and gear as though it were buried treasure. "There's a boat!" she cried breathlessly, pointing on the horizon. "Quick!"

"Yeah, I know," he said in a hollow tone. "I saw it, too."

"Well, hurry up!" She nudged him sharply with her knee. "Get your stuff!"

The angry knot in his throat finally loosened in a few well-chosen words. "Jennifer," he said flatly, "if you'd been paying attention instead of chasing that cat, you would have noticed that the boat is passing this island. It doesn't even see us."

"It does too!" she countered.

Blake sighed, trying to maintain control. "Jennifer . . ."

"What do you call that?" she interrupted, motioning clumsily with her armload of gear.

Blake turned and stared unbelievingly at the boat coming toward them. "Good grief!" he exploded, reeling around and making a mad scramble for his gear.

Jennifer was already climbing down the cliff.

Half-dazed, he followed her out to the tip of the rocky peninsula that was mostly exposed by a low tide. "Thanks" was all he could say, over and over. "Thanks!"

"You can thank me later!" she yelled against the cries of the gulls and ospreys circling overhead. "Just start hollering like you've never hollered before!"

"Jennifer." He stopped in his tracks and gave her a sour look. "I wasn't. . . ." But he didn't finish because it didn't matter after all. He knew— they both knew—that their troubles were almost over. The gleaming white cutter with the red and white maple-leaf flag was coming straight toward them.

"It's the Canadian Coast Guard!" Jennifer could hardly contain her joy. "We're safe! We're safe at last!" she cried.

But Blake couldn't speak. There was so much relief and so many thanks inside of him that he felt as if he might explode. It was almost as though he was dreaming but when they finally boarded the cutter, he knew it was true. They were safe.

"Oh, thank you, sir!" Jennifer was the first to speak to the officer in charge. "Thank you so much!" Tousled and disheveled, she and her brother were unaware of the striking contrast they made amidst the polished deck and gleaming white uniforms of the crewmen curiously encircling them.

The dark, middle-aged captain with kind but intelligent eyes, introduced himself. "I'm Captain Woody," he said, offering them his hand. "And this is Crewman Schissler. He'll help you with your things. Then we'd better find out what's been going on."

"Crewman *who?*" Jennifer cocked her head.

"Schissler, Miss," the smiling young crewman explained. "Sounds like a mouthful of seaweed, doesn't it?"

"Sure does," she agreed.

Blake cringed.

"Well, you can call me Bob if you'd like," the good-looking young man went on, reaching for her gear. "Here, let me help."

Jennifer drew back. "Uh, no," she told him. "I can carry this myself."

The curly-haired sailor shrugged, then led the way into the cabin while Blake hurriedly explained to the officer in change who they were and how they happened to be on the island.

"We are starved, though," Jennifer said as soon as the tempting aroma of hot soup hit her nose.

Blake cleared his throat, embarrassed. "Well, maybe you could spare a sandwich, sir?"

"I think Seaman MacDuff can arrange that," Captain Woody said, motioning to the mess cook who was stirring a large pot of soup in the galley.

"What a cute little dining room," Jennifer said

pleasantly, walking over to the trestle table and sitting down on the bench.

"Mess hall, Jennifer," Blake said under his breath, sitting down beside her and giving her a sharp nudge.

Brushing his words aside, Jennifer busily arranged her gear at her feet beneath the table, then tried to straighten her long, tangled hair. "We're sure glad you saw the signal," she said to the captain finally. "I was scared."

"What my sister is trying to say is that we're sure thankful you saw me on those rocks waving that shirt of mine," he cut in. "I was almost sure you hadn't."

Jennifer prickled. "Hey, wait a minute," she said. "It was *me* they saw. I was in the lighthouse!"

He nudged her quiet and went on. "I'll explain, Jennifer," he said with a tolerant nod to the men. "You can tell Aunt Minnie and your friends about your adventures in the lighthouse when we get back to Gooseberry Island. Right now the Coast Guard needs some facts."

"It was amazing we even saw your signal," the captain told them. "One of the crewmen spotted the flash. It was almost blinding. Caught the sun like a mirror."

"No fooling?" Blake shook his head in amazement. "Just a dirty ol' shirt, too!"

The officer scratched his thick brown hair, perplexed. "I think I'd better get this straight."

"Sure," Jennifer put in. "See, I was in the lighthouse and—"

"Jennifer," Blake said icily, "the lighthouse doesn't have anything to do with it."

104

"Yes it does!" she countered.

Blake gave the crew a quick smile of apology, then went on. "As I was saying—"

"I was in the tower looking for Miss Gray," Jennifer said matter-of-factly, "when I spotted—"

"Miss Gray?" Crewman Schissler came up from behind and sat down beside her. "This story gets more interesting by the minute."

And more embarrassing, Blake thought grimly, wishing his sister would keep her mouth shut for a change.

"Do you like cats, sir?" she asked the handsome young crewman.

The white-clad mate nodded.

"And how about you?" She glanced across the table at the captain, who was shaking his head in bewilderment.

"Why, yes, but. . . ."

"Jennifer," Blake said under his breath, his warning gaze boring down hard upon her, "we can talk about the cat *later.*"

She shrugged and smiled up at the mess cook who was placing steaming bowls of soup before them. "Oh, thank you," she said to the friendly man with a frizz of hair like red lichen. "Do *you* like cats?"

"Very much, lass," replied the salty man with the leathery face. "Back hame in Scotland, we had a bunch o' beasties every autumn and spring, we did."

She listened intently as the old seaman rambled on.

"Uh, Jennifer," Blake said as soon as the man had finished, "maybe the Coast Guard needs to know what happened." He was squeezing her arm now and his words were cool. Precise.

"Oh, yes, I almost forgot!" She smiled and turned to the commanding officer.

Captain Woody was trying to suppress a grin. "Yes," he said, clearing his throat, "now, how *did* you signal?"

"By using the reflector on the old lantern in the tower," she said simply. "It was like a mirror catching the reflection of the sun, wasn't it?"

"Huh?" Blake turned to her in shocked disbelief.

"I *told* you I was in the tower looking for Miss Gray when I saw the boat," she said tartly. "I had to do something."

Everyone was listening intently.

"Dinna stop now, lass." The mess cook set down a plate of sandwiches and prodded her on.

"Well, that's about it." Jennifer shrugged, biting hungrily into the delicious sandwich.

Blake was still staring at his sister in amazement. So it was she who signaled the Coast Guard! It was unbelievable. Almost humiliating.

"What's the matter, Blake?" She gave him a quick jab in the ribs. "Aren't you hungry? I mean, this sure beats berries, huh?"

"Yeah . . . sure." He forced a smile and took a large bite. "Sure."

"How did you end up on Obstruction Island anyway?" the captain asked.

"You mean Grizzly Island?" Jennifer corrected, wiping her mouth with a napkin.

"Grrrizzly Island?" The mess cook rolled his *R*'s and peered from around the galley.

"Uh-huh." She nodded. "What did you call it, sir?"

"Obstruction Island," Captain Woody replied.

"Then . . . that must be its real name, huh?" Blake looked up from his bowl of thick soup and wiped his chin.

"I'll be darned," Jennifer said with a smile. "We just figured it was Grizzly Island on account of the signs."

"Signs?" the captain questioned.

Blake and Jennifer told him about the signs that warned them to keep off because of the renegade grizzly.

Captain Woody shook his head, perplexed. "Our government didn't place those signs there," he told them. "And the warning about a renegade grizzly is ridiculous."

"We finally figured that out," Blake put in, "soon after we discovered the pot farm."

A pan fell in the galley, resounding on the polished deck like a gong. "A *whit?*" The dumbstruck mess cook stood in the doorway. "Whit'r ye blitherin' about?"

"Well," Jennifer began, taking her last spoonful of soup, "you see, we found this field of funny little maplely trees that smelled weird—"

"I'll explain," Blake cut in, turning to the startled crew. He told them everything that had happened during the past few days, from the first moment they had discovered the field of marijuana to the pursuit by the two men with guns and the boat they had seen in the cove the night before.

By this time, the captain had taken out a

notebook and was writing hurriedly. "Did you see their boat clearly enough to describe it?" he asked.

"It was too dark," Blake told him, "but I could tell that it was a fairly large purse seiner."

"And the men? Can you describe them?"

"Not too well," Blake went on, telling him as much as he remembered. "We never really got close enough."

"Thank heavens for that," Jennifer muttered under her breath.

"But, is there anything?" the captain prodded. "Anything at all that might give us a clue? There are hundreds of seiners in these waters."

Blake shook his head, then turned to his sister to see if there was anything she could add. But she wasn't there. "Jennifer?" He glanced around, perplexed.

"I'm right here," she said from under the table.

Under the table? He stooped down and stared unbelieving at his sister, who was messing around with the gear at his feet. *What is she doing under the table?*

A slow heat moved up his neck and this time Blake knew that Jennifer had just gone too far.

Too far. . . .

Fourteen
Telltail Tracks

"What on earth is that strange noise?" the captain asked.

Mortified, Blake watched his sister unzip her sleeping bag and expose a very distressed Miss Gray and her four kittens. "How could you, Jennifer?" he groaned. *"How could you?"*

"I *had* to," she said acidly, lifting the mother cat and snuggling it close. "Poor little things. Do you expect me to leave them to die alone on some desolate island with wild beasts?" She crawled out from under the table with the cat.

"Jennifer, we. . . ." Blake looked up at the wide-eyed crew in total humiliation. He was completely without words. *How could she?* he thought numbly. *How could she do something so stupid!*

Miss Gray leaped out of Jennifer's arms and strutted briskly down the corridor toward the radio room.

"I'm sorry," Blake apologized, watching his sister disappear after the cat. "She's this way sometimes. In fact, it happens a lot."

Schissler and MacDuff were crouching over the sleeping bag nest of kittens. "Aw, the wee souls," the Scotsman purred.

But Blake was scarcely listening. He was burning with humiliation, determined that when they got back to Gooseberry Island, he was going to have to sit down with his sister and have a *long* talk. This was unbelievable! And what was taking her so long?

When Jennifer returned from the radio room, she was carrying the cat and sputtering excitedly. "You'll never believe what I just heard!"

Blake moaned.

"I heard her license number on the marine radio," she exclaimed.

"Jennifer, please," Blake pleaded.

"Whose license number?" Captain Woody cut in.

"Miss Gray's!"

The commanding officer shook his head in confusion. "I don't believe I understand, Miss Carson."

"You won't," Blake put in, hoping to smooth over a situation that was growing worse by the minute. "Don't even try."

"WYZ7075," she went on in earnest. "I heard it, plain as day."

"Och, that's no license numberrr, lass," MacDuff's rolling burr cut in. "Those are the radio call numbers for a boat."

"Jennifer, please. . . ." Blake was tugging on her shirt, trying to get her to sit down and keep quiet.

"Well, it's also her license number." She brushed

Blake aside and showed the crew the tag on Miss Gray's collar. "See? Pearl Gray . . . WYZ7075."

"Pearl Gray?" Crewman Schissler spoke up. "Why, that's the name of a purse seiner that's been fishing these waters recently."

"What?" Blake gasped.

"Where did that cat come from?" Captain Woody stood up quickly.

"We don't know," Jennifer replied, placing the mother cat back with her complaining kittens. "At first we thought she was just a fat abandoned cat, except when she wasn't fat anymore, it didn't make any sense."

"Eh, lass?" The Scotsman had perched his squat and thick frame on the bench beside her.

"She had her kittens," Jennifer explained.

"What's that got to do with it?" Blake asked numbly.

"Well," Jennifer went on, "there had to be a *Mister* Gray, didn't there? And since the island was so isolated, we just figured she came from someplace else."

"Perhaps off a boat?" Captain Woody said with a rueful smile.

"Och!" the salty Scotsman threw up his hands. "A boat cat belongin' to a seiner that's hauling somethin' besides salmon through these waters!"

The captain nodded. "But thanks to these two very alert young people, I think we've found our pot smugglers." He motioned his crew to follow him to the radio room, assuring Blake and Jennifer that they would also notify the family of their rescue.

111

Blake shook his head, dumbfounded. "Did you hear that, Jennifer?" he said to his sister, who was already half under the table again.

"Mmmm?"

"Jennifer," he snorted, "if you'd just. . . ."

"Yeah, Blake?" She sat up and faced him squarely.

"If you'd just quit messing around with those cats, I could. . . ."

"You could what?" she challenged.

"I could say it."

"Say what?"

"Thanks. . . ."